ORCHARD BOOKS
96 Leonard Street, London EC2A 4XD
Orchard Books Australia
32/45·51 Huntley Street, Alexandria NSW 2015
1 84362 214 9
First published in Great Britain in 1997
This edition published in 2003
Copyright © Nicola Smee 1997
The right of Nicola Smee to be identified as
the author and illustrator of this work has been asserted by her
in accordance with the Copyright, Designs and Patents Act, 1988.
A CIP catalogue record for this book is available from the British Library.
Printed in Italy

Freddie gets dressed

Nicola Smee

little ORCHARD

My bear's bare
and so am I.
I think we'd better
get dressed.

Pants for me
and
pants for Bear.

T-shirt for me
and
T-shirt for Bear.

Socks for me
and
socks for Bear.

Trousers for
me and ...
I think a skirt for
Bear today.

Shoes for me
and
shoes for Bear.

Oh, no!
It's back to being
bare, Bear!